RAGGYLUG

A True Story

Ernest Thompson Seton

Retold by Quinn Currie

Illustrated by Susan Heinonen

Contents

Raggylug, or Rag, was the name of a young cottontail rabbit. It was given to him because of his torn and ragged ear, a life-mark that he got in his first adventure. He lived with his mother in Olifant's Swamp, where I made their acquaintance and gathered, in a hundred different ways, the little bits of proof and scraps of truth that at length enabled me to write this history.

Those who do not know the animals well may think I have humanized them, but those who have lived so near them as to know something of their ways and their minds will not think so.

It's true rabbits have no speech as we understand it, but they have a way of conveying ideas by a system of sounds, signs, scents, whisker-touches, movements, and example that answers the purpose of speech; and it must be remembered that though in telling this story I freely translate from rabbit into English, *I repeat nothing that they did not say.*

-Ernest Thompson Seton

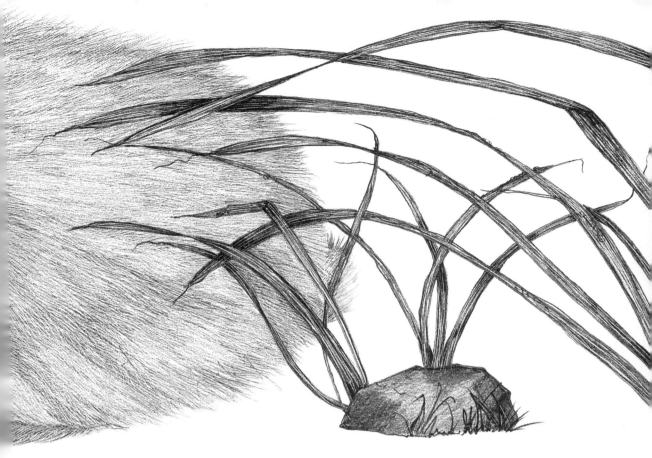

Chapter I
Early Days

Tall swamp grass bent over and concealed the snug nest where Raggylug's mother had hidden him. She had partly covered him with some of the grass, and, as always, her last warning was to "lie low and make no sound, no matter what happens." Though tucked in bed, he was wide awake, and his bright eyes were taking in that part of his little world that was straight above him. A blue jay and a red squirrel, two notorious thieves, loudly berated each other for stealing. Just over Rag's home bush, a yellow warbler caught a blue butterfly six inches from his nose, and later a scarlet and black ladybug, serenely waving her knobbed feelers, took a long walk up one blade of grass, down another, across the nest and over Rag's face, and yet he never moved nor even blinked.

After a while he heard a strange rustling of leaves in the nearby thicket. It was an odd, continuous sound and, although it went this way and that way and came ever nearer, there was no patter of feet with it. Rag had lived his whole life in the swamp (he was three weeks old), and had never heard anything like this before. He became more and more curious. His mother had cautioned him to lie low, but he understood this to mean in case of danger, and he felt that a strange sound without footfalls could not be anything to fear.

The low rasping went past close at hand, then to the right, then back, and seemed to be going away. Rag slowly raised his roly-poly body on his short fluffy legs, lifted his little round head above the covering of his nest, and peeped out into the woods. The sound had ceased as soon as he moved. He saw nothing, so took one step forward for a clear view, and instantly found himself face to face with an enormous black serpent.

"Mommy," he screamed in mortal terror as the monster darted at him. With all the strength of his tiny limbs he tried to run. But in a flash the snake had him by one ear and whipped its coils around him, gloating over the helpless little baby rabbit it had secured for dinner.

2

"Mommy—Mommy," gasped poor little Raggylug as the snake began to choke him. Very soon the little one's cry would have ceased, but bounding through the woods straight as an arrow came Mommy. No longer a shy, helpless little Molly Cottontail, ready to fly from a shadow, she was transformed by the power of mother's love. The cry of her baby had filled her with the courage of a tiger, and—hop, she leapt over that dangerous reptile. Whack, she struck down at it with her sharp hind claws as she passed, giving it such a stinging blow that it squirmed with pain and hissed with anger.

"M-o-m-m-y," came feebly from her little one. And Mommy came leaping again and again, and struck harder and fiercer until the battered reptile let go of the little one's ear and tried to bite the big one as she leaped over.

But all the snake got was a mouthful of wool, and Molly's fierce blows began to tell, as long bloody rips appeared in its black scaly armor.

Things were now looking bad for the snake. Bracing itself for the next charge, the snake lost its tight hold of the baby rabbit, who at once wriggled out of the coils and away into the underbrush, breathless and terribly frightened, but unhurt except that his left ear was much torn by the teeth of the serpent.

Molly had gained all she wanted. She had no notion of fighting for glory or revenge. Off she went into the woods, and the little one followed the shining beacon of her snow-white tail until she led him to a safe corner of the swamp.

Chapter II
Training to Stay Alive

Old Olifant's Swamp was a rough, brambly tract of second growth woods, with a marshy pond and a stream through the middle. A few ragged remnants of the old forest still stood in it, and some huge logs lay about in the brushwood. The land around the pond was of that soggy kind that cats and horses avoid, but that cattle do not fear. The drier zones were overgrown with briers and young trees. The outermost belt of all, next to the fields, was made up of young pines whose needles in the air and on the ground offered a delicious fragrance to the passerby.

The chief inhabitants of the swamp were Molly and Rag. This was their home, where Rag received his training for life.

Molly was a good mother and gave him a careful upbringing. His adventure with the snake taught him the wisdom of the first thing he learned from his mother, to "lie low and say nothing." Rag never forgot that lesson again. He did as he was told, and it made other things come more easily.

The second lesson he learned was "freeze." This lesson grows out of the first, and Rag was taught it as soon as he could run.

"Freezing" is simply doing nothing, turning into a statue. As soon as a well-trained cottontail senses a foe is near, no matter what it is doing, it stays just as it is, stopping all movement; for the creatures of the woods are of the same color as the woods and catch the eye only while moving.

When enemies approach, the one who first sees the other can keep itself unseen by "freezing," and thus have the advantage of choosing the time for attack or escape. Those who live in the woods know the importance of this. Every wild creature must learn it; all learn to do it well, but not one of them can beat Molly Cottontail at it.

Rag's mother taught him this trick by example. When the white cotton cushion of her tail went bobbing away through the woods, Rag ran his hardest to keep up. But when Molly stopped and "froze," he naturally did the same.

8

The best lesson that Rag ever learned from his mother was the secret of the brierbrush. It is a very old secret now, and to make it plain you must first hear why the brierbrush quarrelled with the beasts.

Long ago roses used to grow on bushes that had no thorns. But the Squirrels and Mice would climb after them, the Cattle would knock them off with their horns, the Opossum would twitch them off with its long tail, and the Deer, with its sharp hoof, would break them down.

So the Brierbrush armed itself with spikes to protect its roses and declared eternal war on all creatures that climbed trees, or had horns, or hoofs, or long tails. This left the Brierbrush at peace only with Molly Cottontail, who could not climb, was hornless, hoofless, and had scarcely any tail at all.

In truth the Cottontail had never harmed a brier rose, and having now so many enemies the Brierbush took the Rabbit into a special friendship, and when dangers are threatening, the Rabbit flies to the nearest Brierbrush, certain that here a million keen and sharpened daggers will defend it.

So the secret that Rag learned from his mother was, "The Brierbrush is your best friend."

That season Rag spent much time learning the bramble and brier mazes. He learned them so well that he could go all around the swamp by two different ways and never leave the friendly briers at any place for more than five hops.

Not long ago the foes of the cottontails were disgusted to find that man had brought a new kind of bramble and planted it in long lines throughout the country. It was so strong that no creature could break it down, or chew through it, and so sharp that the toughest skin was torn by it. Each year there was more of it, and each year it became a more serious matter to the wild creatures.

Molly Cottontail had no fear of it. She was not brought up in the briers for nothing. Dogs and foxes, cattle and sheep, and even man himself might be torn by those fearful spikes, but Molly understood it, and lived and thrived under it. The further it spread, the more safe country there was for the cottontail. The name of this new and dreaded bramble is—*the barbed-wire fence.*

Chapter III
Rabbit Language

All season Molly kept Rag busy learning the tricks of the trail, the study of woodcraft, what to eat and drink and what not to touch. Day by day she worked to train him. She taught him little by little, putting into his mind hundreds of ideas that her own life or early training had stored in hers, and so equipped him with knowledge that would keep him safe. Close by her side in the clover field he would sit and copy her when she wobbled her nose to heighten her sense of smell. And he learned that nothing but clear dewdrops from the briers were fit for a rabbit to drink.

As soon as Rag was big enough to go out alone, his mother taught him the signal code. Rabbits telegraph each other by thumping on the ground with their hind feet. A single *thump* means "look out" or "freeze." A slow *thump thump* means "come." A fast *thump thump* means "danger." A very fast *thump thump thump* means "run for your life."

One day, when the weather was fine and the blue jays were quarrelling among themselves, a sure sign that no dangerous foe was about, Rag began a new study. Molly, by flattening her ears, gave the sign for "stay." Then she ran far away and gave the thumping signal for "come." Rag set out and ran to the place but couldn't find Molly. He thumped, but got no reply. Searching carefully, he found her scent. By following this guide, which the animals all know so well and man does not know at all, he worked out the trail and found her. Thus he got his first lesson in trailing. These games of hide and seek became schooling for the serious chases which would come in his later life.

Before that first season of schooling was over he had learned all the principal tricks by which a rabbit lives. He was taught the signs by which to know all his foes, and then the way to baffle them. Hawks, owls, foxes, hounds, minks, weasels, cats, skunks, raccoons, and men, each have a different plan of pursuit; for each of these dangers he was taught a remedy.

And for knowledge of the enemy's approach he depended first on himself and his mother, and then on the blue jay. "Never neglect the blue jay's warning," said Molly. "He is a mischief-maker, but his enemies are our enemies, so pay attention to him."

Rag learned early what some rabbits never learn, that "holing-up" is not always good. It may be safe for a rabbit, but it can also be a deathtrap. A young rabbit always thinks of it first, an old rabbit never tries it till all else fails. It is an escape from a man or a dog, a fox or a bird of prey, but it means sudden death if the foe is a ferret, mink, skunk, or weasel who can fit into the hole.

Chapter IV
The Relay

One bright August morning, sunlight flooded the swamp, soaking everything in a warm radiance. A little brown swamp sparrow was teetering on a
long rush in the pond. Beneath it there were open spaces of water that re-
flected the blue sky and the brilliant yellow duckweed in an exquisite mosaic,
with the bird mirrored in the middle. On the bank behind was a great vigorous
growth of golden green skunk cabbage that cast a dense shadow over the
brown swamp.

The eyes of the swamp sparrow were not made to take in the glorious
colors, but it saw what we might have missed: two of the numberless leafy
brown bumps under the broad cabbage leaves were furry living things, with
noses that never ceased to move up and down when everything else was still.

It was Molly and Rag. They were stretched out under the skunk cabbage because the winged ticks could not stand it there and left them in peace.

Rabbits have no set time for lessons; they are always learning, and their lessons reflect the current problem. They had come to this place for a quiet rest, but suddenly a warning note from the ever-watchful blue jay caused Molly's nose and ears to go up and her tail to tighten to her back. Away across the swamp was Olifant's big black and white dog, coming straight toward them.

"Now," said Molly, "stay here while I go and keep that dog out of mischief." Away she went to meet it, fearlessly dashing across the dog's path.

"Bow-ow-ow," the dog yelped as it bounded after Molly, who kept just beyond its reach, leading it to where a million thorns struck fast and deep, till its tender ears were scratched raw. She guided it at last right into a hidden barbed-wire fence, where it got such a gashing that it went homeward howling with pain.

After making a short double, and a loop in case the dog should come back, Molly returned to find that Rag in his eagerness was standing bolt upright, craning his neck to see the chase. This disobedience made her so angry that she struck him with her hind foot and knocked him over in the mud.

Opportunity for another lesson came one day as they fed on the nearby clover field, and a red-tailed hawk came swooping after them. Molly kicked up her hind legs and skipped into the briers along one of their old trails, where the hawk could not follow. It was the main path from the creekside thicket to the brush pile. Several creepers had grown across it, and Molly, keeping one eye on the hawk, set to work and cut the creepers. Rag watched her, then ran on ahead and cut some more that were across the path. "That's right," said Molly, "always keep the runways clear, you will need them often enough. Not wide, but clear. Cut everything that looks like a creeper across the trail and some day you will find you have cut a snare."

"A what?" Asked Rag, as he scratched his right ear with his left hind foot.

"A snare is something that looks like a creeper, but it doesn't grow and it's worse than all the hawks in the world," said Molly, glancing at the now far away red-tail, "for there it lies night and day in the runway till the chance to catch you comes."

"I don't believe it could catch me," said Rag with the pride of youth. He rose on his heels to rub his chin and whiskers high up on a smooth sapling. Rag did not know why he was doing this, but his mother knew it was a sign, like the changing of a boy's voice, that her little one was no longer a baby but would soon be a grown-up cottontail.

Chapter V
Water Haven

There is magic in running water. Who does not know it and feel it? The thirst parched traveler in the poisonous alkali desert holds back in deadly fear from any pond until he finds one whose center is a thin, clear line with a faint flow, the sign of running, living water; then joyfully, he drinks.

There is magic in running water. The wild wood creature with its deadly foe following tirelessly on its trail, and senses nearing doom feels its strength waning. Its every trick has been tried in vain and then fortune leads it to the running, living water. It dashes in, follows the cooling stream, and with force renewed takes to the woods again.

There is magic in running water. The hounds come to the very spot and halt and cast about, and circle and cast in vain. Their spell is broken by the stream, and the wild thing lives on.

This was one of the great secrets that Raggylug learned from his mother. "After the brierbrush, the water is your next best friend."

One hot, muggy night in August, Molly led Rag through the woods. The white cotton cushion of her tail twinkled ahead and was his guiding lantern, though it went out as soon as she stopped and sat on it. After a few runs and stops to listen, they came to the edge of the pond. The birds in the trees above them were singing *"sleep, sleep,"* and out on a sunken log in the deep water, up to its chin in the cooling bath, a bloated bullfrog was singing the praises of a *"jug o' rum."*

"Follow me," said Molly in rabbit language, and—flop, she went into the pond and struck out for the sunken log in the middle. Rag flinched but plunged in with a little "ouch," gasping and wobbling his nose very fast but still copying his mother. The same movements as on land sent him through the water, and thus he found he could swim. On he went till he reached the sunken log and scrambled up by his dripping mother on the high dry end, surrounded by the water that tells no tales. After this, during warm black nights when that old fox from Springfield came prowling through the swamp, Rag would note the place of the bullfrog's voice, for in case of direst need it might be a guide to safety. From then on, the words of the song that the bullfrog sang were, *"come, come, when in danger, come."*

This was one of the best lessons that Rag learned from his mother; it was really a postgraduate course, for many little rabbits never learn it at all.

Chapter VI
So Many Foes

The cottontails had enemies on every side. Their daily life was a series of escapes. For dogs, foxes, cats, skunks, raccoons, weasels, minks, snakes, hawks, owls, men, and even insects all lived nearby. They had hundreds of adventures, and at least once a day they had to fly for their lives and save themselves by their legs and wits.

Rag was several times chased by the dog, run into the water by the cat, and many times pursued by hawks and owls, but for each danger there was a safeguard. His mother taught him the principal escapes; he improved on them and added many new ones as he grew older. And the older and wiser he grew, the less he trusted to his legs, and the more to his wits for safety.

Ranger was the name of a young hound in the neighborhood. To train him his master used to put him on the trail of one of the cottontails. It was nearly always Rag he chased, for the young buck rabbit enjoyed the runs as much as the dog did, the spice of danger adding zest to the game.

Rag would say, "Oh, mother! Here comes the dog. I'll have a good run today."

"You are too bold, Rag, my son! I fear you will run once too often."

"But mother, it's good training. I'll thump if I'm hard pressed, and you can come and change places with me while I get my second wind."

On Ranger would come, following the trail till Rag tired of it. Then Rag either sent a thumping telegram for help, which brought Molly, or he got rid of the dog by some clever trick.

A description of one of these tricks shows how well Rag had learned the arts of the woods. He knew his scent was strongest near the ground and when he was warm. So if he could get off the ground and be left in peace for half an hour to cool off, while the trail went stale, he knew he would be safe. Therefore, when he tired of the chase, he made for the creekside brier patch, where he zigzagged until he left a course so crooked that the dog was sure to be greatly delayed in working it out. He then went straight to D in the woods, passing one hop to windward of the high log E. Stopping at D, he followed his back trail to F, where he leaped aside and ran toward G. Then, returning on his trail to J, he waited till the hound passed on his trail at I.

Rag then got back on his old trail at H, and followed it to E, where, with a great leap aside, he reached the log; running to its high end, he sat like a bump.

Creekside Thicket

Ranger, as planned, lost time in the bramble maze, and the scent was poor when he got it straightened out and came to D. Here he began to circle to pick it up, and after losing much time, found the trail which ended suddenly at G. Again he had to circle to find the trail. Wider and wider he circled, until at last he passed right under the log Rag was on. However, a cold scent, on a cold day, does not go downward much. Rag never budged nor winked, and the hound passed.

Again the dog came around. This time he crossed the low part of the log, and stopped to smell it. Yes, clearly it was rabbity, but it was a stale scent now. Still, Ranger mounted the log.

It was a trying moment for Rag, as the great hound came sniff-sniffing along the log. But his nerve did not forsake him. The wind was right; he had his mind made up to bolt as soon as Ranger came halfway up.

But he didn't come. Another dog might have seen the rabbit sitting there, but the hound did not. The scent seemed stale, so he leaped off the log. Rag had won again.

Chapter VII
A Challenger

Rag had never seen any rabbit other than his mother. Indeed, he had scarcely thought about there being any other. He was more often away from her now, and yet he never felt lonely, for rabbits do not hanker for company. One day in December, while he was among the red dogwood brush, cutting a new path to the great creekside thicket, he saw all at once against the sky over Sunning Bank the head and ears of a strange rabbit.

The newcomer had the air of a well-pleased discoverer and soon came hopping Rag's way along one of *his* paths into *his* swamp. A new feeling rushed over Rag, that boiling mixture of fear and envy called jealousy.

The stranger stopped at one of Rag's rubbing trees; that is, a tree against which he would stand on his heels and rub his chin as far up as he could reach. He thought he did this simply because he liked it; but all buck rabbits do so, and several ends are served. It makes the tree rabbity, so that other rabbits know that this swamp already belongs to a rabbit family and is not open for settlement. It also lets the next passing rabbit know by the scent if the last caller was an acquaintance; the height from the ground of the rubbing places shows how tall the rabbit is.

Now to his disgust, Rag noticed that the newcomer was a head taller than himself, a big, stout buck. This was a wholly new experience for Rag and filled him with a curious new feeling. Hopping forward onto a smooth piece of ground, he struck slowly:

Thump—thump—thump, which is a rabbit telegram for, "get out of my swamp, or fight."

The newcomer made a big V with his ears, sat upright for a few seconds, then, dropping on his forefeet, sent along the ground a louder, stronger, *thump—thump—thump.*

And so war was declared.

They came together by short runs sideways, each one trying to tire the other and watching for the chance of an advantage. The stranger was a big, heavy buck with plenty of muscle; however, one or two mistakes showed that he had not much cunning, and counted on winning his battles by his weight.

He charged again, and Rag met him in a fury. As they came together they leaped up and struck out with their hind feet. *Thud—thud,* and Rag went down. In a moment the stranger was on him; he was bitten, and lost several tufts of hair before he could get up.

Rag was the swifter of foot and managed to get out of reach. Again the stranger charged, and again Rag was knocked down and bitten severely. He was no match for his foe, and it soon became a question of saving his own life.

Although he was injured, Rag sprang away with the stranger in full pursuit, bound to oust him from the swamp where he was born. Rag's legs and wind were good, but the stranger was big and heavy, and soon had to give up the chase. But on that day, a reign of terror began for Rag. His training had been against dogs, weasels, hawks, men, and such, but he didn't know what to do when chased by a rabbit. He chose to lie low till he was found, then run.

One day a goshawk came swooping over the swamp, and the stranger, while keeping under cover, tried to drive Rag into the open. Once or twice the hawk nearly had him, but by reaching the briers Rag escaped.

Raggylug had just about made up his mind to leave the swamp with his mother and go into the world in search of a new home when suddenly he heard old Thunder the hound, sniffing and searching about the swamp. He resolved to play a desperate game, and deliberately crossed the hound's view. The chase that began was fast and furious.

Three times around the swamp they went, till Rag had made sure that his mother was hidden safely and his hated foe was in his usual nest. Then right into that nest and over him he jumped, giving him a rap with one hind foot as he passed over his head.

The stranger jumped up, only to find himself between Rag and the dog, and heir to all the perils of the chase.

Thunder came on, baying hotly on the scent just ahead. The buck's weight and size, while great advantages in a rabbit fight, were now fateful. He did not know many tricks, just the simple ones like "double," "wind," and "hole-up." The chase was too close for doubling and winding, and he didn't know where the holes were.

The baying of the hound and the crashing of the brush were borne to Rag and Molly where they crouched in hiding. Suddenly these sounds stopped; there was a scuffle, then silence.

Rag knew what the silence meant. It sent a shiver through him, but he soon recovered, realizing he was master of the swamp once more.

Chapter VIII
Clearing the Swamp

The Olifants had started to burn all the brush piles to the east and south of the swamp, and to clear up the wreck of the old barbed-wire hog pen just below the spring.

During the January thaw, they cut the rest of the large wood around the pond, which curtailed the cottontails' domain on all sides. It was hard on Rag and his mother. The brush piles were their various residences and outposts, and the barbed-wire their safe retreat. They had lived in the swamp for so long that they felt it to be their very own, every trail, every brier patch and hiding place.

They clung to the dwindling swamp. It was their home, and they wanted to stay in it. Their life was filled with daily perils, but they were still fleet of foot, long of wind, and bright of wit.

They were somewhat troubled by a mink that had recently wandered upstream to their quiet nook. For the present they gave up using the ground holes, which were dangerous blind alleys against a mink.

The first snow was gone, and the weather turned bright and warm. Molly was somewhere in the lower thicket. Rag was sitting in the weak sunlight on a bank. The smoke from the familiar gable chimney of Olifant's house came drifting in a pale blue haze through the woods, showing as a dull brown against the brightness of the sky. The sun-gilt gable was cut off midway by the banks of brierbrush which, purple in the shadows, shone like rods of blazing crimson and gold in the light. Beyond the house, the barn with its gable and roof stood up like a wooden ship.

The sounds that came from it, and the delicious smell that mingled with the smoke told Rag that the animals were being fed cabbage in the yard. Rag's mouth watered at the idea of the feast. He blinked and blinked as he sniffed its fragrant promises, for he loved cabbage dearly. But he had been to the barnyard the night before after a few paltry clover tops, and no wise rabbit would go two nights running to the same place.

Therefore, he did the wise thing. He moved across where he could not smell the cabbage and made his supper of a bundle of hay that had been blown from the stack. Later, when about to settle for the night, he was joined by Molly, who had taken her teaberry and then eaten her frugal meal of sweet birch near the Sunning Bank.

Chapter IX
Danger

The sun had gone about its business elsewhere, taking all of its gold and glory along. Off in the east a big black cloud appeared and rising higher and higher spread over the whole sky, shutting out all light. Then the wind, taking advantage of the sun's absence, came on the scene and set about brewing trouble. The weather turned colder and colder; it seemed worse than when the ground had been covered with snow.

"Isn't it terribly cold? I wish we still had our stovepipe brush pile," said Rag.

"A good night for the pine-root hole," replied Molly, "but we have not yet seen that mink's nesting spot, and it is not safe till we do."

The hollow hickory was gone—in fact at this very moment its trunk, lying in the wood-yard, was harboring the mink they feared. So the cottontails hopped to the south side of the pond and, choosing a brush pile, they crept under and snuggled down for the night; they faced the wind, but with their noses in different directions so as to go out different ways in case of alarm.

The wind blew harder and colder as the hours went by, and about midnight a fine icy snow came ticking down on the dead leaves and hissing through the brush heap. It might have seemed a poor night for hunting, but the old fox from Springfield was out. He came pointing up the wind in the shelter of the swamp and chanced into the lee of the brush pile, where he scented the sleeping cottontails. He halted for a moment, then came stealthily sneaking up toward the brush under which his nose told him the rabbits were crouching. The noise of the wind and the sleet enabled him to come quite close before Molly heard the faint crunch of a dry leaf under his paw. She touched Rag's whiskers, and both were fully awake just as the fox sprang on them. They always slept with their legs ready for a jump.

Molly darted out into the blinding storm. The fox missed his spring but followed like a racer, while Rag dashed off to one side.

There was only one road for Molly, straight up the wind; bounding for her life she gained a little over the unfrozen mud that would not carry the fox, till she reached the edge of the pond. No chance to turn now, on she must go.

Splash, through the weeds she went, plunging into the deep water. And the fox plunged in close behind. It was too much for the fox on such a night; he turned back. Molly struggled through the reeds to deeper water, striking out for the other shore. There was a strong headwind. The waves, icy cold, broke over her head as she swam, and the water was full of snow that blocked her way like soft ice. The dark line of the shore seemed far away, and perhaps the fox was waiting there.

She laid her ears flat to be out of the gale and bravely put forth all her strength, with wind and tide against her. She had nearly reached the farthest reeds when a great mass of floating snow barred her way.

She struck out, slowing with each stroke. When at last she reached the lee of the tall reeds, her limbs were numbed, her strength spent, her brave little heart was sinking. Through the reeds she passed, but once in the weeds her course wavered; her feeble strokes sent her landward, but her limbs were too cold and weak to escape the fox, should he be there.

There was no fox waiting for her. Rag had escaped the first onset of the foe, and as soon as he regained his wits he came running back to help his mother. He met the old fox going around the pond to meet Molly and led him far away, then dismissed him with a barbed-wire gash on his head.

Rag came to the bank and sought about, thumping for Molly with no reply. He saw her at last, chilled and exhausted, but safe on shore. Rag found a root hole where the two of them snuggled down again. Molly rested, satisfied that Rag had learned his lessons well.

Raggylug continued to live in the swamp. Old Olifant died that winter, and the unthrifty sons ceased to clear the swamp or mend the wire fences. Within a single year it was a wilder place than ever; fresh trees and brambles grew, and falling wires made many cottontail castles and last retreats that dogs and foxes dared not storm. Rag became a big strong buck who feared no rivals. He had a large family of his own, and a pretty brown wife that he met I know not where. There, no doubt, his children's children will flourish for many years to come. There you may see them any sunny evening if you have learned their signal code, choose a good spot on the ground, and know just how and when to thump it.